*To Tom and Dov, as always,
and to Cindy and my friends.*

CHAPTER ONE

Bagels and Beans

Hi. Remember me? I'm Josh Bernstein, the kid with a dog named Bagels.

It's Monday morning, and Dad's making breakfast.

"Who's up for baked beans in tomato sauce on a toasted bagel?" he asks, holding up the can of Betsy Brown's Baked Beans.

My sister, Becky, and I shout out, "We are!"

It's our favorite breakfast food.

Bagels begins to drool. He also loves Betsy Brown's Baked Beans.

"No, Bagels," Dad says. "I'm sorry, but this is only for humans."

For reasons I won't go into, we try to keep beans away from Bagels. But it's actually the sauce he likes best. That's why I let him lick the dirty plates before they go into the dishwasher. Actually, we all like the sauce best.

Bagels's other favorite foods are turkey sausages, underwear, old socks and, of course, bagels.

Our cat, Creamcheese, prefers to eat Cat Banquet. According to the TV ads, it's *the canned food for cats with good taste.*

Lox, our goldfish, only eats dried bugs. I guess he *doesn't* have such good taste.

"You know," Dad says to Becky and me, "you guys ought to be on a television commercial for these baked beans."

I don't want to be on TV, but Becky does. And I'm sure Bagels does too. He's an actor.

Becky smiles at a nonexistent camera and mimics the TV ad.

"Betsy Brown's Baked Beans are the world's favorite. It's all in the sauce."

"Weroof," barks Bagels as he turns the dog version of a cartwheel.

That's when Mom rushes into the kitchen.

She's waving a letter.

"Can you guess what this is?" she says.

We're all about to guess, but she doesn't give us time.

"We're going on a cruise," she says. "This letter is from the Betsy Brown's Baked Beans company."

What a coincidence!

"Remember the contest I entered?" says Mom. "I had to write about why my family loves Betsy Brown's Baked Beans in tomato sauce?"

No one remembers, but we all nod.

"I won. A week's family cruise to California *and* a year's supply of baked beans."

"A year's supply of baked beans," I say. "Now that's what I call a prize."

"Of course, we'll give some of the baked beans to the food bank," says Mom.

No one argues. We think the whole world should be able to enjoy Betsy Brown's Baked Beans.

"What's a cruise?" asks Becky.

"A cruise," says Mom, "is a relaxing week on a ship. You usually stop at different ports. But our cruise ship, the *Princess Belinda,* doesn't make stops. She only goes to San Francisco and back."

Mom puts down the letter. I pick it up.

"It sounds boring," says Becky.

"It'll be fun. There are kids' programs," says Mom.

"I don't like kids' programs. They never do stuff I want to do."

"There's an all-you-can-eat buffet," I say. I point at the letter in my hand. "Becky, you like buffets."

"Who doesn't?" says Dad, as he dishes up the bagels and beans.

Becky says that she'd prefer to go to the Amazon.

I really don't know why my parents let Becky watch documentaries on the Knowledge Network. They give her ideas.

"Too dangerous," Mom says. "You might get lost in the Amazon. It's a jungle out there."

Then Becky says, "Can Lox, Bagels and Creamcheese come along?"

"Aunt Sharon will take care of the house and the pets, like she did when we went camping," says Dad.

"Bagels came camping with us," says Becky.

"That was different," says Mom.

I look down at Bagels. He grins. He executes a backflip.

"We can't leave Bagels behind. He'll get into trouble without us."

Dad says Aunt Sharon will make sure he behaves.

I doubt it.

Bagels has personality, but he doesn't always take instructions very well.

He's a mix of sheltie, whippet and Jack Russell. That's a wild combination. He's also an escape artist. Sometimes Creamcheese helps him open doors and windows. She likes to get him into trouble.

Becky and I have been training Bagels. We've cured him of barking when he shouldn't. He doesn't round up joggers anymore, and he usually comes when called. Except when he doesn't feel like it. But without Becky and me to keep an eye on him, he could easily have a relapse.

"No pets allowed on this cruise," says Mom. "Unless they're seeing-eye dogs or other helping animals."

"Bagels can be helpful," says Becky. "You could say he's our nanny, like Nana in *Peter Pan*."

As I mentioned before, Bagels is an actor. *Peter Pan* was his first show. His second was *Pup in Boots*.

"No one would believe Bagels is your nanny," says Mom.

"Even in a uniform?" asks Becky.

"Especially in a uniform," says Mom. "Listen, I love Bagels as much as you do. And if we could take him, I would."

"Becky's right," I say. "Bagels can be helpful."

I remind them that Bagels rescued Dad from the lake when we went camping. "*And* he gave him CPR."

"Yes," says Becky. "What if Dad falls overboard on the *Princess Belinda*?"

"Don't worry," says Mom. "I'll keep an eye on Dad."

"That's a relief," says Dad.

Later I ask Becky, "How much trouble can Bagels get into in a week?"

Becky looks at me as if to say, *You're kidding, right?*

CHAPTER TWO

The Princess Belinda

"Have you got everything?" asks Aunt Sharon.

She and Bagels have come to see us off at the docks.

Bagels is restless. He sniffs the air. It smells of gasoline, seaweed and barnacles.

I show Aunt Sharon my suitcase and my camera.

"*I've* got everything," I say.

I look up at the *Princess Belinda*. She's big.

Becky asks me, "Are you sure this will float?"

"Sure," I say.

Becky's only six. I don't tell her that I once read a book about a ship called the *Titanic*. It didn't have a happy ending.

Becky says she's going to wear her yellow plastic water wings the whole trip.

Bagels pulls on the leash and leaps up at me.

Dad says, "Bagels, please behave while we're away."

Bagels cocks his head to one side.

Dad can't really get angry with a dog that saved his life.

He scratches Bagels behind the ears.

"We'll be back soon, Bagels."

Bagels dances a jig and does a backflip. He doesn't realize he's not coming with us.

"Get on board, already," says Aunt Sharon. "I want to treat myself to brunch." She points to a fancy hotel next to the docks.

"Lock Bagels in the car," says Mom. "They won't allow him in the dining room."

Becky nods. "He'd eat all the turkey sausages."

Dad reminds Aunt Sharon not to let Bagels anywhere near baked beans while we're away.

Aunt Sharon salutes. "Message received and understood."

"Time to board," says Dad. Everyone heads for the *Princess Belinda*.

Before I follow, I whisper to Aunt Sharon.

"Bagels loves the tomato sauce more than the beans."

"Okay," says Aunt Sharon. "I'll let him lick my plate."

We high-five.

I head for the ship.

I turn one last time. Aunt Sharon waves. Bagels isn't smiling.

I take a photo.

"Poor Bagels," Becky says.

We wave. Bagels wags his tail. But it's a pretty weak wag, if you ask me.

"We have a suite!" Mom is beaming.

It looks like a palace to me. Two big bedrooms—one with a massive bed, the other with two singles. There are two bathrooms *and* my parents have a hot tub.

"This is like a *movie* set," says Mom.

There's a basket on Mom and Dad's bed. It's full of fruit, chocolates and… two cans of beans.

"Well," says Dad. "They certainly laid on the luxury."

Becky says maybe this trip won't be so bad after all.

Whoot, whoot!

The ground moves.

"Anchors aweigh!" says Dad. "We're off."

CHAPTER THREE

Lunch with Captain Spiggot

We've been invited to have lunch at the captain's table.

Captain Spiggot wears a white uniform. He's trying to pretend that Becky isn't wearing water wings.

"I'm Captain Horatio Spiggot," he says. "Welcome to the *Princess Belinda*." He looks at Becky and me.

"And how are you young people enjoying everything so far?"

Becky asks if it's possible to get lost on the ship.

The captain says no.

"Don't be afraid, young lady. We are at sea. Sooner or later, lost people get found."

Becky hates being called *young lady*.

"Oh, I'm not afraid," she says. "I was hoping it might be like the jungle."

The captain looks confused.

Dad snorts.

"What a lovely ship," says Mom, changing the subject.

Over at the buffet table, Becky and I pile food on our plates.

We sit down again. I'm just about to eat some baked beans when my phone vibrates.

Mom glares at me.

It's a text from Aunt Sharon.

SOS. Bagels escaped from car while I was eating delicious but expensive brunch. I'll send updates later. But DON'T TELL YOUR PARENTS.

"Oh no," I say.

Mom asks what's wrong.

I put away the phone.

"Just Aunt Sharon. She lost something, but I think she'll find it."

Dad raises an eyebrow. "And she thought you should know?"

I shrug. "Aunt Sharon and I are very close."

I try not to worry about Bagels. He always finds his way home.

I check out the other passengers. There are some families, like ours. Also, there are lots of really old people.

"You kids are going to have fun," says the captain. "Wait until you see the kids' entertainment lineup. Face painting, treasure hunts, Hula-Hoop contests. We pull out all the stops on the *Princess Belinda*."

Becky kicks me under the table.

"Hey!" I yell.

Mom glares again.

"Hey," I say again, in a normal voice. "That sounds like fun. I can't wait. Can you, Becky?"

Becky gives me another of her looks. This one says, "I can wait."

CHAPTER FOUR

Espionage
(That Means Spies and Stuff)

I check out the passengers again. Now I see they're not all families or old folks. For instance, there's a guy in dark glasses and a trench coat nearby. He looks like a spy. I take his photo. *Snap.*

There's another guy across the room with thick blond hair. The hair looks fake. He's also wearing dark glasses. Another spy? I call him Blondie. *Snap.*

Farther across the room there's a woman sitting alone. She's wearing a brown-and-red dress. She's eating baked beans and salami. Her hair is an unusual shade of red. It reminds me of something. I can't remember what, but I decide to call her Red.

I'm sure I've seen her face before.

But where? It'll come to me later. *Snap*.

Wait a minute. Am I dreaming? Is that a trail of sausages disappearing behind a pillar? (This ship has lots of pillars.)

I blink. The sausages aren't there anymore. I could be mistaken. I look at the last photo on my camera.

I wasn't mistaken. There's a sausage about to disappear behind the pillar.

I'd like to investigate, but Mom wants to take a tour of the ship.

The *Princess Belinda* is big.

I don't care what anyone says. You
could easily get lost on this thing.

People stare at Becky's water wings.
Becky stares right back.

I'm sure someone's following us. I turn around. I see something move behind a potted palm tree.

Why would anyone follow *us*?

On the way back to our suite, I see Red. She's talking to a guy at the concierge's desk. She gives him an envelope. He nods, then puts it in a safe.

Red smiles and walks away.

That's when I spot Blondie. He's behind a pillar. He's looking at Red through a pair of tiny opera glasses.

He's up to something for sure.

Is he the one who's been following us?

Is he the one stealing sausages?

Snap.

Maybe this cruise won't be so boring after all. I might catch a spy. I could be like James Bond.

If only Bagels were here to help me.

CHAPTER FIVE

He Is!

At dinnertime, the buffet table has even more food on it. It looks pretty fancy. There's even a sculpture made of ice. It looks like a bridge.

"That's the Golden Gate Bridge," Mom says. "We'll see it when we arrive in San Francisco." *Snap*.

After dinner we watch a cabaret in a room like a nightclub. Mom and Dad order a round of Shirley Temples.

I tell the waiter I want mine shaken, not stirred.

First in the cabaret is a guy who does magic tricks. He's followed by a man who tells jokes that I don't understand.

Finally, a guy dressed like Elvis leaps onto the little stage and sings "Hound Dog." Dad hums along. He's a big Elvis fan. So is Bagels. It's the one thing they have in common. In fact, Bagels likes to howl along when Elvis is singing on the car radio.

"Wooo, hoo, hoo…"

What was that?

"Wooo, hoo, hoo…"

I look at Mom. I look at Dad. They haven't heard it.

I check out the audience. No one else has heard it either. I must be imagining things.

After the show we go back to the suite.

We're all pretty tired.

Becky and I get into our beds.

Becky's going to sleep in her water wings.

Mom's so tired she only reads one book to Becky and me.

"Let's call it a day," she says.

"It's a day," says Becky, then she's out cold and snoring.

Scritch, scritch.

I wake up in the middle of the night. I hear scratching.

Why is there a porthole in my bedroom?

Then I remember. I'm on a cruise.

Scritch, scratch.

There's that sound again. It's coming from the door.

I sit up. Becky is still snoring.

I tiptoe to the door.

Silence.

I peep through the little spyhole. No one there.

I yawn and go back to bed.

Scritch, scratch, tap. I wake up again.

Now the scratching is coming from the porthole.

How can that be? Then I remember— of course, the porthole's fake. It looks out onto a deck, not the sea.

I climb out of bed again.

I tiptoe over to the fake porthole. I look out.

Bagels grins at me.

CHAPTER SIX

Hiding Bagels

I open the porthole. Bagels leaps into my arms. He licks my face. He starts to make a yipping sound. I shake my head.

"No, Bagels. Do...not...bark. Say nothing," I whisper, "or we are doomed."

He seems to understand.

"Oh, Bagels," I whisper, giving him a big kiss, "it really was you singing with Elvis."

I listen at my parents' door. It's quiet. Mom and Dad are asleep.

I wake Becky.

She sees Bagels. She's about to shriek with joy. I put my fingers to my lips. She nods.

Bagels is licking Becky's face. She hugs him.

I tell Becky about the text from Aunt Sharon.

"How did he sneak on board?" she whispers.

"I don't know," I say. "But Creamcheese couldn't have helped him this time."

"Should we tell Mom and Dad?"

"No," I say. "I hate lying, but we'll be in big trouble if anyone finds out. We have to hide Bagels."

Becky looks around. "Where?"

"Under my bed for now," I tell her. "In the morning, I can carry him around in my backpack till the cleaning people have finished with the rooms. We'll sneak him food from the all-you-can-eat buffet. It has all the stuff he loves. Except for socks and underwear."

"But what about when Bagels has to go to the bathroom?" says Becky.

"The newspaper," I say. "Captain Spiggot says it gets delivered every day. Mom and Dad won't notice. They never read tabloids."

Bagels curls up under my bed.

"Do you think we should get Bagels some water wings?" asks Becky.

"Don't you remember?" I say. "Bagels can swim."

She grins.

She remembers.

I've figured out who's been following me today. And those disappearing sausages at breakfast yesterday? Bagels for sure.

CHAPTER SEVEN

Bagels on Board

In the morning, I wake up early. I hear Mom and Dad.

"Hey, kids," Mom shouts through the door. "Have your showers. We'll meet you at breakfast."

"Becky," I whisper, "the cleaning people will be here soon. We'll take Bagels to breakfast and bring him back when the coast is clear."

As soon as Mom and Dad leave, I sneak into their room. I take the front page of the newspaper.

Bagels understands what it's for. He smiles, then demonstrates.

Becky and I wait until he's done. We scrunch the front page into a plastic bag, then pop it into the garbage can.

Bagels climbs into my backpack.

As we make our way to the morning buffet, Bagels wiggles in the backpack. A man stares at me.

At least he's not staring at Becky's water wings.

"I have trouble keeping still," I tell him. It's not a lie. I do have trouble keeping still. I execute a jig. Bagels would be proud. The man shakes his head and walks away.

We reach the dining room. I spot Mom and Dad. They're at a table in the middle. I sneak a few pastrami slices and some turkey sausages from the buffet.

I stuff them into the top of the backpack. Bagels snaps them from my hands and gives me a thank-you lick.

A woman stares at me.

"It's a snack for later," I say.

I sit down and stow my backpack under the table.

Mom asks why I'm carrying my backpack around with me.

"Emergency supplies," I say.

She doesn't look convinced.

Dad asks Becky if she plans to wear water wings for the whole week.

Becky says yes.

Dad nods. "Good plan." He pours himself another coffee.

Bagels doesn't bark even once.

It seems too good to be true.

CHAPTER EIGHT

009

So far so good. I've figured out what time the cleaning people finish with our suite every morning. That's when Becky and I sneak Bagels back to our room.

Up until now, Becky and I have managed to avoid all the shipboard activities. Instead, we follow Blondie and Trench Coat. *They* seem to be following Red.

I think I'm on to something.

I'm sure Red is a government agent.

Obviously, those were secret documents that she put in the ship's safe. Blondie and Trench Coat are spies out to steal the secrets.

I decide it will be my job to save the country. I'll call myself 009—because 007 is already taken, and I'm nine. Too bad Bagels is in hiding. I know he'd

come in handy now that he's almost trained.

It's not easy trying to save the country when you're only nine—even 009. Stuff gets in the way. For example:

"My, Mrs. Bernstein. And the young Bernsteins." Captain Horatio Spiggot has accosted my mother. (*Accost* is a word I read in a book once. It means to stop someone in their tracks.) She's in a hurry to get to a dance class. (It's not just kids who are programmed on a cruise.)

"I must say, Mrs. Bernstein, I couldn't help observing that your children certainly have hearty appetites," he says.

"What do you mean?" says Mom.

"They're always taking food from the buffet—which is what it's there for, after all. Bagels, pastrami and, of course, their favorite."

Mom looks blank.

"Turkey sausages," says the captain.

"Sausages?" says Mom.

The captain frowns. He's obviously thinking, What kind of mother is this, who doesn't know her kids' favorite food?

Mom makes a quick recovery.

"I knew that," she says.

He tips his hat and walks away to accost another family.

Obviously, accosting is part of his job.

Mom looks at us suspiciously.

"You both hate sausages."

"It's like this," I say, thinking fast. "Remember how I hated avocados when I was little, and then one morning I woke up and I loved them?"

"So?"

"Well, it's the same with sausages. We both hated them, and now we love them."

Becky smiles and nods.

Mom says, "You hated them last week."

"That was then," says Becky.

"This is now," I add.

Mom says, "As far as I know, the only member of this family who loves turkey sausages is Bagels. And he's back at home."

Bagels hears his name and begins to wiggle.

"Darling." Dad appears, looking very smart in a tux.

"We don't want to be late for fox-trot lessons," he says.

Dad looks at me.

"You and Becky should head over to the Children's Activity Room. Today is clowning."

"I'm scared of clowns," Becky says.

"But this is different," says Dad. "This time *you* get to be the clown."

"What if I scare myself?" says Becky.

I grab my sister's hand and pull her away.

I steer her toward the Children's Activity Room.

"Just keep walking, Becky. We don't *have* to be clowns. We'll do something else."

In half an hour, we can safely lock Bagels in the cabin.

We've reached one of the sitting areas. It's full of those potted palm trees and pillars. We flop down on a sofa.

"I need to think," I tell Becky.

Before I can think, I hear voices coming from behind the nearest palm plant.

"The secret is in that safe. I know it is. I saw her put it there," says a guy.

"Are you sure that's what it is? It could be anything."

"Like what? No. That information is too important to put in an email. It's the secret, all right. We'll steal it and make a fortune."

"How much do you think the other guys will pay us?" asks guy number two.

"A lot," says guy number one.

I peek between the palm fronds.

I might have guessed it.

Trench Coat and Blondie.

They're talking about Red.

I was right. She *is* a government agent.

I look at Becky. She's heard everything. Her eyes are very wide.

Meanwhile, the backpack's wiggling.

As the two spies get up and walk away, Bagels growls.

"Grrr."

It's the first word he's said in days.

Becky grabs my arm. She knows Bagels only growls when he senses trouble. He senses these guys are Trouble.

Time to head back to the cabin.

Bagels races around our room a few times. He does a backflip. Then he chases his tail.

"Those guys talked like spies on TV," says Becky.

"And Bagels growled," I remind her. "Bagels is never wrong." We're both remembering the Sasquatch at the lake.

"But what's that government lady doing on a cruise?"

"She's on a secret mission," I tell her. "The spies followed her. Those papers are very important, Becky."

We leave Bagels with a bowl of water and the sports section from the newspaper.

"Remember, Bagels—don't say a word." Bagels runs around the room one more time. He crashes under Becky's bed. He snores. But not as loud as Becky.

We avoid the clowning lesson.

Becky still wants to get lost, but I tell her she has to help me save the country.

"Perhaps even the world."

"If you insist," she says.

We look in on Mom and Dad. They've finished with the fox-trot. Now they're doing a tango. Mom has a rose between her teeth. We try to track down Blondie and Trench Coat, but they're in hiding. We see Red doing laps in the pool. Government agents have to keep in good shape.

That night there's a formal dinner.

Mom makes me wear a suit with a bow tie. It's not comfortable, but I remind myself that James Bond also dresses for dinner.

Becky's wearing a pink dress with sequins all over it. Aunt Sharon made it for her. It clashes with the green water wings.

Before dinner, we get official photographs taken in front of more palm trees and pillars.

It's steak for dinner. When no one is looking, I put some in a ziplock bag for Bagels. I know he'll be thrilled.

He is.

CHAPTER NINE

Missing Secrets

Next morning, I get to breakfast first. I see Blondie and Trench Coat. They're sitting at adjoining tables.

Blondie is reading a newspaper upside down, and Trench Coat is texting.

Very suspicious. I take photos.

I check out Red. She's eating scrambled eggs with baked beans.

Mom, Dad and Becky arrive.

"Josh," says Mom, "you're not eating your turkey sausages. You have ten of

them on your plate. I thought they were your new favorite food."

They're really for Bagels, but I can't avoid it. I have to eat one, or Mom will be suspicious. I chew it very slowly.

When no one's looking, I slip two sausages to Bagels. I put the rest of them in a ziplock bag and slip it into my pocket. Just in time.

"Wow," says Dad, looking at my empty plate. "That was quick."

Mom says, "You didn't have to wolf them down, Josh."

Bagels burps. I say, "Excuse me."

"Joshua Bernstein," says Mom. "Let that be a lesson not to eat so fast."

My phone vibrates. It's Aunt Sharon.

Still no Bagels! Where can he be? Creamcheese appears very happy. Lox looks a bit depressed.

I reply:

Bagels managed to sneak on board. We are hiding him. Parents don't know. We are on a spy mission. Please don't tell. Josh xxx

Aunt Sharon answers:

Thank goodness for that. I think.

And don't worry, your secret is safe with me. The question is, how long can Bagels be kept under wraps?

Over and out.

PS. Good luck with the spy thing.

Mom wants to know who's texting me now.

"It's Aunt Sharon. Everything's fine."

Mom gives me a squinty look. Dad raises his eyebrows.

I have such suspicious parents.

"So," says Dad, "what are today's activities for you children?"

I tell him there's a treasure hunt. "It sounds like a lot of fun," I say. "Doesn't it, Becky?"

I kick her lightly under the table.

"Sure does," Becky says. Her smile is good. It almost convinces *me*.

Mom and Dad seem satisfied.

"I hope Aunt Sharon's not having any problems with Bagels," says Mom.

"She isn't," I tell her.

Mom and Dad are going for a swim in the pool. Then they've got an advanced fox-trot lesson, followed by a tango master class.

"After that," says Dad, "we'll have a quiet afternoon in the hot tub, listening to music."

At least our parents will be out of the way while we save the world.

CHAPTER TEN

Treasure

"We have to get Bagels back to the cabin, so we don't miss the treasure hunt."

Becky looks horrified. "You mean we have to go on the treasure hunt? I thought we were going to catch bad guys."

I really want to find those spies, but if we keep avoiding kids' activities, Mom and Dad are sure to find out.

The second we let Bagels free in the room, he dances around. He's the one who should take fox-trot lessons. He yips a few times, until I give him the sign to be quiet. He snaps his jaw shut, waiting for further instructions.

I grab the food and fashion page from my parents' room. That's when I catch a glimpse of those cans of baked beans in the basket. I pick one up. I examine it closely.

"What do you know," I say to myself.

I put the can back. Now I'm really confused.

As we leave the cabin, I look around. Something seems different, but I'm not sure what. I have an uneasy feeling. Becky drags me away, and we head for the Children's Activity Room.

As we pass the concierge's desk, I see Red.

She's upset.

"But I gave it to you for safekeeping," she says.

"The envelope has vanished, Miss. I swear, I don't know how it disappeared."

I stop.

The bad guys broke into the safe and stole the secrets.

"We have to find Blondie and Trench Coat," I tell Becky.

Becky's eyes light up. "You mean we're not going on the treasure hunt?"

"This is more important than a treasure hunt, Becky…"

Then I stop. I have an idea.

"We'll pretend we're on the treasure hunt," I say. "That way we'll blend in with the other kids. The spies won't be suspicious."

The children's-activity leader is called Bob. He's wearing a blue blazer. He says,

"Well, children, are you all ready for the treasure hunt?"

Everyone says, "Yes, Bob."

He explains the rules.

"Take a name tag. Wear it at all times. Find a partner. No one should be wandering around alone. Over on that table are copies of the first clue. Each clue leads to the next and so on. If you have any problems, you can ask one of the entertainment stewards." He points to a group of stewards.

They also wear blue blazers.

I read the first clue out loud.

"*A message lies behind the palms*
Look for the lady with no arms."

Becky makes a face.

"Gross."

But I understand the clue.

I hold Becky's hand. "Let's go," I say.

We run along a corridor, then turn a corner.

There it is. Between two of those potted palm trees. A plaster statue of a woman with no arms.

"Quick," I say to Becky. "There must be another clue."

Then I stop in my tracks.

"Yarooo. Rruff, weroof, yaroo."

Becky and I look at each other.

"Bagels," we say together.

Then we see Blondie and Trench Coat. They run past the end of the corridor. Bagels is in hot pursuit.

"Aarf, aarf, yaroo."

That's when I remember what looked odd in our room. The person who cleaned it must have opened the fake porthole. Bagels escaped.

I'll probably be grounded for the next five years.

But not until I save the free world.

"Quick, Becky," I say. "We have to follow Bagels."

It's not easy keeping up with Bagels. He's gaining on Blondie and Trench Coat.

Blondie stops briefly. He puts his hand inside a potted palm. He starts running again.

Bagels also stops. He puts his muzzle inside the pot. Next second, he's got something in his mouth. Then he sets off after the spies again.

"Help!"

I look behind us. It's Red.

"Stop those men," she calls to us. "They've stolen the secret."

Maybe if I'm a hero and save the country, I *won't* get grounded for five years.

We pass another corridor. A few treasure-hunt kids are searching behind potted palms. There's an entertainment steward with them.

The steward looks up and sees Bagels.

"A dog!" he yells. "There's an illegal dog on board the ship!"

He takes out a whistle and blows it.

"Dogs are not allowed on this ship. Stop, I say!"

We run past him.

I just hope that Mom and Dad are in the hot tub. I hope they're listening to loud music and can't hear any of this.

Blondie and Trench Coat are about to turn another corner when Becky trips and falls.

Bang, bang! Her water wings burst.

Trench Coat stops in his tracks. He puts up his hands.

"Don't shoot," he yells.

Blondie crashes into a potted palm tree. His hair falls off. I told you it was a wig.

He grabs it and puts it on backward.

"I surrender," he says.

I help Becky up from the deck.

"My wings burst," she howls. "What if we sink?"

I give her a hug. "We won't," I say, trying not to think of the *Titanic*.

Becky points at Bagels.

"What's Bagels got in his mouth?"

I look closely.

It's an envelope.

Red takes it from him.

"It's my recipe," she says. "Good dog." She pats Bagels's head.

Bagels does a backflip.

"Recipe?" I say.

"Inside this envelope is my new, improved baked-beans recipe," she says.

"These two men are employed by Norris Norton's Baked Beans Company.

They make the second most popular baked beans in the world. They wanted to steal my new recipe so they could be number one. They broke into the safe and took it. Your dog sniffed them out."

"You look familiar," says Becky.

I tell her, "It's Betsy Brown. Her face is on all the cans of beans. At first I thought you were a government agent, Miss Brown."

Miss Brown smiles at me. "You are quite the detective," she says. "And call me Betsy. Everyone does. You and your sister deserve a reward."

Bagels barks and does a backflip.

Betsy pats him.

"Of course. You deserve a reward too." She looks at me again. "So what'll it be?"

"Well, first, could you tell the captain about how Bagels is really a helping dog? After all, he did help us catch the thieves."

"Sure thing," says Betsy. "But you must want something else."

"Could I get back to you on that?" I ask.

"Take all the time you need," says Betsy.

Becky, Bagels and I go out on deck. Just in time.

We're sailing under the Golden Gate Bridge.

It looks even better than the one carved out of ice.

I take out my camera. *Snap*.

We take a detour to the gift shop. Becky needs new water wings.

Finally, the three of us are in the cabin.

Becky says, "What reward should we ask for, Josh?"

"*I* don't really want anything," I say. "We're already getting a year's supply of baked beans. But I have an idea."

I explain my plan. Becky hugs me. I knew she'd approve.

I tell Betsy Brown my idea. She likes it. She also explains about Bagels to the captain.

"So really, captain," she says, "that dog is a hero."

Then she talks to Mom and Dad.

They agree not to ground me. This time.

"By the way," I say to Betsy when we're alone, "why do you always wear a red-and-brown dress?"

She smiles. "And don't forget the hair," she says, patting her own head.

She leans closer and whispers, "I dress in the colors of my product. People take one look at me and think…"

"Baked beans in tomato sauce," I say.

"But don't tell anyone," she says. "It can be our little secret."

"I promise."

CHAPTER ELEVEN

A Commercial Break

A month later, we're in our sitting room. Mom switches on the TV. We're all pretty excited—especially Becky and Bagels.

My sister appears on the screen. She's happily eating a plateful of baked beans. A man's voice says, "Your children will love Betsy Brown's Baked Beans in the New and Improved Tomato Sauce."

The TV Becky stops eating and grins.

"This new recipe is yummy," she says from the screen. She holds up a can of beans.

And there's Betsy Brown's face on the label.

The shot changes. Now Bagels is onscreen. He's eating from a bowl of dog food. There's a can beside the bowl.

Real Bagels leaps onto my lap. He barks at his TV image.

The man's voice says, "And now Betsy Brown has created Canine Supreme dog food, rich in tomato sauce. A meal no dog can resist."

There's a close-up of the can.

Only this time, it isn't Betsy Brown on the label.

This time it's Bagels Bernstein—star of stage and screen.

Real Bagels does a backflip on my lap.

"Bagels," I say. "You are a ham! But I love you."

He licks my face.